Dear Parents and Educators,

P9-CQT-267

Welcome to Penguin Young Readers! As parents and educators, you know that each child develops at his or her own pace—in terms of speech, critical thinking, and, of course, reading. Penguin Young Readers recognizes this fact. As a result, each Penguin Young Readers book is assigned a traditional easy-to-read level (1–4) as well as a Guided Reading Level (A–P). Both of these systems will help you choose the right book for your child. Please refer to the back of each book for specific leveling information. Penguin Young Readers features esteemed authors and illustrators, stories about favorite characters, fascinating nonfiction, and more!

A Is for Amber What a Trip, Amber Brown	LEVEL **3** GUIDED READING LEVEL **L**

This book is perfect for a **Transitional Reader** who:
- can read multisyllable and compound words;
- can read words with prefixes and suffixes;
- is able to identify story elements (beginning, middle, end, plot, setting, characters, problem, solution); and
- can understand different points of view.

Here are some **activities** you can do during and after reading this book:
- Compare/Contrast: Amber and Justin are two characters in this story. Make a list of words that describe each of them. How are they alike? How are they different?
- Discuss: How did Amber feel when Justin splashed her in the pool? How do you think Justin felt after he splashed Amber?
- Make Predictions: What do you think the families will do during the rest of their vacation? What will Amber do when her dad tries to do work on Monday?

Remember, sharing the love of reading with a child is the best gift you can give!

—Bonnie Bader, EdM, and Katie Carella, EdM
   Penguin Young Readers program

*Penguin Young Readers are leveled by independent reviewers applying the standards developed by Irene Fountas and Gay Su Pinnell in *Matching Books to Readers: Using Leveled Books in Guided Reading*, Heinemann, 1999.

To Margaret Frith—PD

Penguin Young Readers
Published by the Penguin Group
Penguin Group (USA) Inc., 375 Hudson Street, New York, New York 10014, USA
Penguin Group (Canada), 90 Eglinton Avenue East, Suite 700, Toronto, Ontario M4P 2Y3, Canada
(a division of Pearson Penguin Canada Inc.)
Penguin Books Ltd., 80 Strand, London WC2R 0RL, England
Penguin Group Ireland, 25 St. Stephen's Green, Dublin 2, Ireland (a division of Penguin Books Ltd.)
Penguin Group (Australia), 250 Camberwell Road, Camberwell, Victoria 3124, Australia
(a division of Pearson Australia Group Pty. Ltd.)
Penguin Books India Pvt. Ltd., 11 Community Centre, Panchsheel Park, New Delhi—110 017, India
Penguin Group (NZ), 67 Apollo Drive, Rosedale, Auckland 0632, New Zealand
(a division of Pearson New Zealand Ltd.)
Penguin Books (South Africa) (Pty.) Ltd., 24 Sturdee Avenue,
Rosebank, Johannesburg 2196, South Africa

Penguin Books Ltd., Registered Offices: 80 Strand, London WC2R 0RL, England

Text copyright © 2001 by Paula Danziger. Illustrations copyright © 2001 by Tony Ross. All rights
reserved. First published in 2001 by G. P. Putnam's Sons and Puffin Books, imprints of Penguin Group
(USA) Inc. Published in 2011 by Penguin Young Readers, an imprint of Penguin Group (USA) Inc.,
345 Hudson Street, New York, New York 10014. Manufactured in China.

The Library of Congress has cataloged the G. P. Putnam's Sons edition
under the following Control Number: 99055555

ISBN 978-0-698-11908-6   10 9 8 7 6 5 4 3 2 1

IS FOR AMBER

What a Trip, Amber Brown

by Paula Danziger
illustrated by Tony Ross

Penguin Young Readers
An Imprint of Penguin Group (USA) Inc.

"I scream. You scream. We all
scream for ice cream." Justin and I
sing over and over again.

Danny just screams, "Ice cream!
Ice cream! Ice cream!" Danny
is only three. He is Justin's little
brother.

"That's enough," Mom says. We are going on vacation for two whole weeks—I, Amber Brown, my mom, Justin, who is my best friend, Danny, and their mom, Mrs. Daniels. Our dads are coming up on the weekend. That's when their vacations start.

We're almost in the Poconos. That's where the house is.

"Poke a nose." Justin pretends
to poke me in the nose.

"Poke a nose." I, Amber Brown,
poke back.

"Ice cream in the nose." Danny giggles behind us.

"Justin and Amber, you are going to be second-graders in a few weeks," my mom says. "I expect you to be more grown-up. You know that the Poconos is an area in Pennsylvania. Now settle down until we get there."

Justin and I make blowfish faces
at each other. Then we hear a really
disgusting sound behind us. We
can't turn around. We are wearing
seat belts. We can't see anything, but
we sure can smell it.

Mrs. Daniels pulls off the road. She cleans Danny up. Justin and I do not poke our noses, we hold them. The van smells yucky.

We drive some more. Then Mom says, "Turn right—we're almost there!" We drive up to a big white house.

"We're here!" My mom sounds very happy.

Justin and I jump out and run around. There's a tree with a swing. Behind the fence we find a swimming pool.

This is going to be one amazing-great vacation—as soon as we get unpacked!

I, Amber Brown, am the fastest
unpacker in the world. In just seven
and three-quarter minutes, all
of my things are put away. Justin
knocks, comes in, and looks around.

"You are so lucky not to have to
share your room with a puke-head
brother." Then he says, "Come on,
slowpoke. Let's go outside. If you
don't hurry up, I'm going to have to
poke a slow in the poke-a-nose."

"Justin Daniels," I say, "we just got here a few minutes ago."

"Well, I finished unpacking and I have been waiting for you, Amber."

"First, I have to see your room," I say. I want to find out how Justin has become the fastest unpacker in the world. I find out. Justin Daniels is the messiest unpacker in the world.

We go downstairs and our moms
give us bananas. Justin and I pretend
to be monkeys. We scratch under
our arms.

We run around. We find
a tree house . . . we can pretend
it's a monkey house. The pool . . .
we can be whales.

An animal with antlers watches us from the woods.

"Oh, dear—a deer," I say. "Maybe it belongs to Santa and it's on vacation."

Justin starts singing, "Rudolph the red-nose reindeer . . ." And then he hits himself in the nose. "That's why his nose is red . . . because he is a poke-a-nose." The deer leaves.

"Justin," I say, "let's have a sleep-out." We've had sleep-overs, but NEVER a sleep-out.

He jumps up and down. "Great idea!" Now all we have to do is convince our parents.

"It's okay if your father will sleep out with you," my mom says.

"Ask your dad when he calls tonight," Justin's mom tells him.

"Let's go swimming in the pool," Danny says. Actually, Justin and I call it the swimming "ool" because our moms told us that there must not be any pee in the pool. I hope that they keep reminding Danny.

"Splash!" Danny says, jumping into the water.

Danny has been able to swim since he was a baby. So has Justin.

I, Amber Brown, am afraid to swim. But I like being in the pool as long as my feet touch the bottom and I wear a life jacket.

Justin swims back and forth. He splashes me.

"Stop that," I say. Justin doesn't.

He splashes me again. Water goes up my nose.

"Submarine attack," Justin shouts. He ducks down and comes up. He sprays a mouthful of water at me.

"I said STOP!" I yell.

"Scaredy-cat baby." He sticks out
his tongue.

"I'm not a baby." I splash him. He
splashes back. Now a whole gallon
of water goes up my nose. I cough.
The water comes out of my nose.

Justin gets out and does a cannonball. *SPLASH!*

I, Amber Brown, am totally mad. His mom yells at him. I, Amber Brown, am glad.

Wait until we're on dry land at our sleep-out. When a giant grizzly bear attacks I will save us, and Justin Daniels will have to say that I, Amber Brown, am the bravest person in the world. Until then, I will not talk to him.

I, Amber Brown, am staying in my room, reading. I am not talking to Justin. I am not talking to my mom, because she said that I should talk to Justin.

I look out my window and see the "ool," which is now probably a pool because of Danny.

I hate not talking to people. But I've told everyone that I am mad.

There's a knock on the door.

"Who's there?" I ask.

"Boo." It's Justin's voice. I say nothing. He repeats, "Boo."

"Two boos make a boo-boo, and that's what you made . . . a boo-boo on our friendship," I say.

"Amber. Come on," he pleads. "Boo."

"Boo who?" I finally say. He opens the door.

"You don't have to cry. I'm sorry," he says. Justin makes a fish face at me.

"I don't want to see anything that has to do with water right now." I fold my arms in front of me.

Justin gets down on his hands and knees and makes puppy-dog sounds.

"Roll over. Play dead," I say. He does. Then he crawls over, licks my hand, and lies down again. I can't help myself. I scratch him on his tummy like he's a dog. It's hard to stay angry at Justin.

I, Amber Brown, am so excited. So is Justin Daniels. Our dads are here and as soon as it gets dark, we are going to have a sleep-out.

Danny is not as excited as we are. He has to stay in the house with our moms. We told him he is having a "sleep-in," but he's no dope. He knows that's just a way of saying, "You're a baby and can't do what the big kids are doing."

Justin and I have made a pile of things that we really need.

Our dads are putting up the tent.
Our moms are packing the "grub."
Justin and I have already packed
some of our own grub.

It starts to get dark. Justin's father
comes back to the house.

"The tent's ready." He has a bump
on his head from the tent falling
over on him.

Justin and I jump up. Danny yells, "I want to go."

"No," Justin and I say together. Danny falls to the ground and has a major temper tantrum.

We grab our things and head for the tent. We can still hear Danny yelling. My father is standing by the tent. He is on his cell phone.

"Mike. Please tell the client that I will be in touch Monday morning." I drop some of the camping stuff on his foot.

"Oops."

My father moves his foot and keeps talking.

"Dad," I say. "This is your vacation. It's our vacation."

He looks down at me. I give him
that look that says, "I am your
daughter . . . your only child . . .
please oh please . . . do this for me."
He says, "Good-bye. Talk with you
on Monday. I have some camping
on my calendar right now."

On Monday, I will give him that
look again.

We put everything away and then have dinner. Justin and I make hot-dog kebabs with onions, little tomatoes, and marshmallows. We all sit around singing songs and TV ads.

Then the ghost stories start. Our
dads can tell some very scary stories.

I don't know about Justin's tummy . . .
but mine is beginning to hurt. I don't
know if it's the kebabs
or the scary stories.

It's getting darker. The lightning bugs are flashing. I wonder what animals are out at night in the Poconos.

"Time to go to sleep," my dad says.
Just before I get into my sleeping
bag, Justin says, "We'd better check to
make sure there are no snakes in our
bags." I, Amber Brown, check very
carefully.

Then I get into my sleeping bag.
Our fathers get into their bags. They
go to sleep very quickly. They snore
very loudly.

It's hard to go to sleep with
two noses snoring at once. I keep
hearing sounds outside. I, Amber
Brown, am getting very nervous.

"Amber," Justin whispers. "Do you
hear that noise?" I listen.

At first I hear nothing and then I hear a tiny *"Grrrrrrrrrrrrrr."* It's a grizzly bear. I just know it.

I remember how brave I thought I would be if a grizzly bear attacked us. Well, duh, I'm scared of the grizzly bear, too.

"Grrrrrrrrrrrrrr." I hear it again.

I see Justin put his head inside his
sleeping bag. I do the same in mine.

I hear someone laughing. It does not sound like a grizzly-bear laugh. It sounds like a Danny Daniels giggle. I poke my head out of the sleeping bag. It is Danny, and he doesn't have any clothes on.

Danny's father wakes up, reaches over, grabs his little boy, and tickles him. Then he puts a shirt on him.

We weren't attacked by a grizzly bear . . . we were attacked by a bare Danny.

"I snucked out," he says.

Mr. Daniels has his arms around
Danny. He looks happy to be there.

We take a vote. Danny gets to stay
with us. My dad phones the house to
let our moms know.

Our moms come out and join us.
I, Amber Brown, already know that
there is no place like home. Now I,
Amber Brown, know that there is no
place like tent.